MW01253629

*I care.*
*May this pure and simple message of*
*hope lift you up today.*

*To:* _____

*From:* _____

*Date:* _____

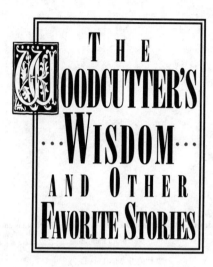

# THE WOODCUTTER'S WISDOM AND OTHER FAVORITE STORIES

# MAX LUCADO

WORD PUBLISHING
Dallas · London · Vancouver · Melbourne

**The Woodcutter's Wisdom and Other Favorite Stories by Max Lucado**

Published by Word Publishing

© 1995 by Max Lucado

All rights reserved. No part of this publication may be reproduced,
stored in a retrieval system, or transmitted in any form or by any
means—electronic, mechanical, photocopy, recording, or
any other—except for brief quotations in printed reviews,
without the prior permission of the publisher.

"The Woodcutter's Wisdom" is taken from
*In the Eye of the Storm* © 1991 by Max Lucado; "The Sweet Song of the
Second Fiddle" from *When God Whispers Your Name* © 1994 by Max
Lucado; "The Cave People" and "The Yay-Yuck Man" from
*A Gentle Thunder* © 1995 by Max Lucado.
ISBN 08499-5214-X

Printed in the United States of America

For information about "UpWords" radio
ministry featuring Max Lucado, write:

P. O. Box 5860
San Antonio, TX 78201

## Introduction

· · · · · · ·

**I**LOVE STORIES. I love reading them, and better still, I love writing them. Stories help us understand biblical truths in a fresh way. Sometimes they help us see ourselves more objectively, through the lens of the imagination.

I've gathered a few of my favorite stories in this booklet. I hope they remind you of what being a child of God is all about. May you enjoy them as much as I enjoyed writing them!

*Chapter One*
. . . . . . .

# The Woodcutter's Wisdom

WOULD YOU buy a house if you were only allowed to see one of its rooms? Would you purchase a car if you were permitted to see only its tires and a taillight? Would you pass judgment on a book after reading only one paragraph?

Nor would I.

Good judgment requires a broad picture. Not only is that true in purchasing houses, cars, and books, it's true in evaluating life. One failure doesn't make a person a failure; one achievement doesn't make a person a success.

"The end of the matter is better than its beginning,"[1] penned the sage.

"Be . . . patient in affliction,"[2] echoed the apostle Paul.

"Don't judge a phrase by one word," stated the woodcutter.

The woodcutter? Oh, you may not know him. Let me present him to you.

I met him in Brazil. He was introduced to me by a friend who knew that I needed patience. Denalyn and I were six months into a five-year stint in Brazil, and I was frustrated. My fascination with Rio de Janeiro had turned into exasperation with words I couldn't speak and a culture I didn't understand.

"Tenha paciência," Maria would tell me. "Just be patient." She was my Portuguese instructor. But, more than that, she was a calm voice in a noisy storm. With maternal persistence, she corrected my pronunciation and helped me learn to love her homeland.

Once, in the midst of a frustrating week of trying to get our goods out of customs (which eventually took three months), she gave me this story as a homework assignment. It helped my attitude far more than it helped my Portuguese.

It's a simple fable. Yet for those of us who try to pass judgment on life with only one day's evidence, the message is profound. I've done nothing to embellish it; I've only translated it. I pray that it will remind you, as it did me, that patience is the greater courage.

❧

Once there was an old man who lived in a tiny village. Although poor, he was envied by all, for he owned a beautiful white horse. Even the king coveted his treasure. A horse like this had never been seen before—such was its splendor, its majesty, its strength.

People offered fabulous prices for the steed, but the old man always refused. "This horse is not a horse to me," he would tell them. "It is a person. How could you sell a person? He is a friend, not a possession. How could you sell a friend?" The man was poor and the temptation was great. But he never sold the horse.

One morning he found that the horse was not in the stable. All the village came to see him. "You old fool," they scoffed, "we told you that someone would steal your horse. We warned you that you would be robbed. You are so poor. How could you ever hope to protect such a valuable animal? It would have been better to have sold him. You could have gotten whatever price you wanted. No amount would have been too high. Now the horse is gone, and you've been cursed with misfortune."

The old man responded, "Don't speak too quickly. Say only that the horse is not in the stable. That is all we know; the rest is judgment. If I've been cursed or not, how can you know? How can you judge?"

The people contested, "Don't make us out to be fools! We may not be philosophers, but great philosophy is not needed. The simple fact that your horse is gone is a curse."

The old man spoke again. "All I know is that the stable is empty, and the horse is gone. The rest I don't know. Whether it be a curse or a blessing, I can't say. All we can see is a fragment. Who can say what will come next?"

The people of the village laughed. They thought that the man was crazy. They had always thought he was a fool; if he wasn't, he would have sold the horse and lived off the money. But instead, he was a poor woodcutter, an old man still cutting firewood and dragging it out of the forest and selling it. He lived hand to mouth in the misery of poverty. Now he had proven that he was, indeed, a fool.

After fifteen days, the horse returned. He hadn't been stolen; he had run away into the forest. Not only had he returned, he had brought a dozen wild horses with him. Once again the village people gathered around the woodcutter and spoke. "Old man, you were right and we were wrong. What we thought was a curse was a blessing. Please forgive us."

The man responded, "Once again, you go too far. Say only that the horse is back. State only that a dozen horses returned with him, but don't judge. How do you know if this is a blessing or not? You see only a fragment. Unless you know the whole story, how can you judge? You read only one page of a book. Can you judge the whole book? You read only one word of a phrase. Can you understand the entire phrase?

"Life is so vast, yet you judge all of life with one page or one word. All you have is a fragment! Don't say that this is a blessing. No one knows. I am content with what I know. I am not perturbed by what I don't."

"Maybe the old man is right," they said to one another. So they said little. But down deep, they knew he was wrong. They knew it was a blessing. Twelve wild horses had returned with one horse. With a little bit of work, the animals could be broken and trained and sold for much money.

The old man had a son, an only son. The young man began to break the wild horses. After a few days, he fell from one of the horses and broke both legs. Once again the villagers gathered around the old man and cast their judgments.

"You were right," they said. "You proved you were right. The dozen horses were not a blessing. They were a curse. Your only son has broken his legs, and now in your old age you have no one to help you. Now you are poorer than ever."

The old man spoke again. "You people are obsessed with judging. Don't go so far. Say only that my son broke his legs. Who knows if it is a blessing or a curse? No one knows. We only have a fragment. Life comes in fragments."

It so happened that a few weeks later the country engaged in war against a neighboring country. All the young men of the village were required to join the army. Only the son of the old man was excluded, because he was injured. Once again the people gathered around the old man, crying and screaming because their sons had been taken. There was little chance that they would return. The enemy was strong, and the war would be a losing struggle. They would never see their sons again.

"You were right, old man," they wept. "God knows you were right. This proves it. Your son's accident was a blessing. His legs may be broken, but at least he is with you. Our sons are gone forever."

The old man spoke again. "It is impossible to talk with you. You always draw conclusions. No one knows. Say only this: Your sons had to go to war, and mine did not. No one knows if it is a blessing or a curse. No one is wise enough to know. Only God knows."

The old man was right. We only have a fragment. Life's mishaps and horrors are only a page out of a grand book. We must be slow about drawing conclusions. We must reserve judgment on life's storms until we know the whole story.

I don't know where the woodcutter learned his patience. Perhaps from another woodcutter in Galilee. For it was the Carpenter who said it best:

"Do not worry about tomorrow, for tomorrow will worry about itself."[3]

He should know. He is the Author of our story. And he has already written the final chapter.

*Chapter Two*

. . . . . . .

# The Sweet Song of the Second Fiddle

F OR THOUSANDS of years, the relationship had been perfect. As far back as any one could remember, the moon had faithfully reflected the sun's rays into the dark night. It was the greatest duo in the universe. Other stars and planets marveled at the reliability of the team. Generation after generation of earthlings were captivated by the reflection. The moon became the symbol of romance, high hopes, and even nursery rhymes.

"Shine on, harvest moon," the people would sing. And he did. Well, in a way he did. You see, the moon didn't actually shine. He reflected. He took the light given to him by the sun and redirected it toward the earth. A simple task of receiving illumination and sharing it.

You would think such a combo would last forever. It almost did. But one day, a nearby star planted a thought in the moon's core.

"It must be tough being a moon," the star suggested.

"What do you mean? I love it! I've got an important job to do. When it gets dark, people look to me for help. And I look to the sun. He gives me what I need and I give the people what they need. People depend on me to light up their world. And I depend on the sun."

"So, you and the sun must be pretty tight."

"Tight? Why, we are like Huntley and Brinkley, Hope and Crosby, Benny and Day . . ."

"Or maybe Edgar Bergen and Charlie McCarthy?"

"Who?"

"You know, the man and the dummy."

"Well, I don't know about the dummy part."

"That's exactly what I mean. You are the dummy. You don't have any light of your own. You depend on the sun. You're the sidekick. You don't have any name for yourself."

"Name for myself?"

"Yeah, you've been playing second fiddle for too long. You need to step out on your own."

"What do you mean?"

"I mean stop reflecting and start generating. Do your own thing. Be your own boss. Get people to see you for who you really are."

"Who am I?"

"Well, you are, uh, well, uh, well, that's what you need to find out. You need to find out who you are."

The moon paused and thought for a moment. What the star said made sense. Though he had never considered it, the moon was suddenly aware of all the inequities of the relationship.

Why should he have to work the night shift all the time? And why should he be the one the astronauts stepped on first? And why should he always be accused of making waves? And why don't the dogs and wolves howl at the sun for a change? And why should it be such an outrage to "moon" while "sunning" is an accepted practice?

"You are right!" asserted the moon. "It's high time we had a solar-lunar equity up here."

"Now you're talking," prodded the star. "Go discover the real moon!"

Such was the beginning of the breakup. Rather than turning his attention toward the sun, the moon began turning his attention toward himself.

He set out on the course of self-enhancement. After all, his complexion was a disgrace, so full of craters and all. His wardrobe was sadly limited to three sizes; full-length, half-cast, and quarter-clad. And his coloring was an anemic yellow.

&

So, girded with determination, he set out to reach for the moon.

He ordered glacier packs for his complexion. He changed his appearance to include new shapes such as triangular and square. And for coloring he opted for a punk-rock orange. "No one is going to call me cheese-faceanymore."

The new moon was slimmed down and shaped up. His surface was as smooth as a baby's bottom. Everything was fine for a while.

Initially, his new look left him basking in his own moonlight. Passing meteors would pause and visit. Distant stars would call and compliment. Fellow moons would invite him over to their orbits to watch "As the World Turns."

He had friends. He had fame. He didn't need the sun—until the trends changed. Suddenly "punk" was out and "prep" was in. The compliments stopped and the giggles began as the moon was slow to realize that he was out of style. Just as he finally caught on and had his orange changed to pinstripe, the style went to "country."

It was the painful poking of the rhinestones into his surface that caused him to finally ask himself, "What's this all for anyway? You're on the cover of the magazine one day and forgotten the next. Living off the praise of others is an erratic diet."

For the first time since he'd begun his campaign to find himself, the moon thought of the sun. He remembered the good ol' millenniums when praise was not a concern. What people thought of him was immaterial since he wasn't in the business of getting people to look at himself. Any praise that came his way was quickly passed on to the boss. The sun's plan was beginning to dawn on the moon. "He may have been doing me a favor."

He looked down upon the earth. The earthlings had been getting quite a show. They never knew what to expect: first punk, then preppie, now country. Oddsmakers in Las Vegas were making bets as to whether the next style would be chic or macho. Rather than be the light of their world he was the butt of their jokes.

Even the cow refused to jump over him.

But it was the cold that bothered him the most. Absence from the sunlight left him with a persistent chill. No warmth. No glow. His full-length overcoat didn't help. It couldn't help; the shiver was from the inside, an icy shiver from deep within his core that left him feeling cold and alone.

Which is exactly what he was.

One night as he looked down upon the people walking in the dark, he was struck by the futility of it all. He thought of the sun. *He gave me everything I needed. I served a purpose. I was warm. I was content. I was . . . I was what I was made to be.*

Suddenly, he felt the old familiar warmth. He turned and there was the sun. The sun had never moved. "I'm glad you're back," the sun said. "Let's get back to work."

"You bet!" agreed the moon.

The coat came off. The roundness returned, and a light was seen in the dark sky. A light even fuller. A light even brighter.

And to this day whenever the sun shines and the moon reflects and the darkness is illuminated, the moon doesn't complain or get jealous. He does what he was intended to do all along.

The moon beams.

*Chapter Three*

· · · · · · ·

# The Cave People

L ONG AGO, or maybe not so long ago, there was a tribe in a dark, cold cavern. The cave dwellers would huddle together and cry against the chill. Loud and long they wailed. It was all they did. It was all they knew to do. The sounds in the cave were mournful, but the people didn't know it, for they had never known joy. The spirit in the cave was death, but the people didn't know it, for they had never known life.

But then, one day, they heard a different voice. "I have heard your cries," it announced. "I have felt your chill and seen your darkness. I have come to help."

The cave people grew quiet. They had never heard this voice. Hope sounded strange to their ears. "How can we know you have come to help?"

"Trust me," he answered. "I have what you need."

The cave people peered through the darkness at the figure of the stranger. He was stacking something, then stooping and stacking more.

"What are you doing?" one cried, nervous.

The stranger didn't answer.

"What are you making?" one shouted even louder.

Still no response.

"Tell us!" demanded a third.

The visitor stood and spoke in the direction of the voices. "I have what you need." With that he turned to the pile at his feet and lit it. Wood ignited, flames erupted, and light filled the cavern.

The cave people turned away in fear. "Put it out!" they cried. "It hurts to see it."

"Light always hurts before it helps," he answered. "Step closer. The pain will soon pass."

"Not I," declared a voice.

"Nor I," agreed a second.

"Only a fool would risk exposing his eyes to such light."

The stranger stood next to the fire. "Would you prefer the darkness? Would you prefer the cold? Don't consult your fears. Take a step of faith."

For a long time no one spoke. The people hovered in groups covering their eyes. The fire builder stood next to the fire. "It's warm here," he invited.

"He's right," one from behind him announced. "It's warmer." The stranger turned and saw a figure slowly stepping toward the fire. "I can open my eyes now," she proclaimed. "I can see."

"Come closer," invited the fire builder.

She did. She stepped into the ring of light. "It's so warm!" She extended her hands and sighed as her chill began to pass.

"Come, everyone! Feel the warmth," she invited.

"Silence, woman!" cried one of the cave dwellers. "Dare you lead us into your folly?

Leave us. Leave us and take your light with you."

She turned to the stranger. "Why won't they come?"

"They choose the chill, for though it's cold, it's what they know. They'd rather be cold than change."

"And live in the dark?"

"And live in the dark."

The now-warm woman stood silent. Looking first at the dark, then at the man.

"Will you leave the fire?" he asked.

She paused, then answered, "I cannot. I cannot bear the cold." Then she spoke again. "But nor can I bear the thought of my people in darkness."

"You don't have to," he responded, reaching into the fire and removing a stick. "Carry this to your people. Tell them the light is here, and the light is warm. Tell them the light is for all who desire it."

And so she took the small flame and stepped into the shadows.

# Chapter Four

# The Yay-Yuck Man

**B**OB LOVED to make people happy. Bob lived to make people happy. If people weren't happy, Bob wasn't happy. So every day Bob set out to make people happy. Not an easy task, for what makes some people happy makes other people angry.

Bob lived in a land where everyone wore coats. The people never removed their coats. Bob never asked *Why?* He only asked *Which?* "Which coat should I wear?"

Bob's mother loved blue. So to please her he wore a blue coat. When she would see him wearing blue she would say, "Yay, Bob! I love it when you wear blue." So he wore the blue coat all the time. And since he never left his house and since he saw no one but his mother, he was happy, for she was happy and she said "Yay, Bob" over and over.

Bob grew up and got a job. The first day of his first job he got up early and put on his best blue coat and walked down the street.

The crowds on the street, however, didn't like blue. They liked green. Everyone on the street wore green. As he walked past, everyone looked at his blue coat and said, "Yuck!"

Yuck! was a hard word for Bob to hear. He felt guilty that he had caused a "yuck" to come out of a person's mouth. He loved to hear "yay!" He hated to hear "yuck!"

When the people saw his blue coat and said "yuck," Bob dashed into a clothing store and bought a green coat. He put it on over his blue coat and walked back out in the street. "Yay!" the people shouted as he walked past. He felt better because he had made them feel better.

When he arrived at his workplace, he walked into his boss's office wearing a green coat. "Yuck!" said his boss.

"Oh, I'm sorry," said Bob, quickly removing the green coat and revealing the blue. "You must be like my mother."

"Double yuck!" responded the boss. He got up from his chair, walked to the closet, and produced a yellow coat. "We like yellow here," he instructed.

"Whatever you say, sir," Bob answered, relieved to know he wouldn't have to hear his boss say "yuck" anymore. He put the yellow coat over the green coat, which was over the blue coat. And so he went to work.

When it was time for him to go home, he replaced the yellow coat with the green and walked through the streets. Just before he got to his house, he put the blue coat over the green and yellow coats and went inside.

Bob learned that life with three coats was hard. His movements were stiff, and he was always hot. There were also times when the cuff of one coat would peek out and someone would notice, but before the person could say "yuck" Bob would tuck it away.

One day he forgot to change his coat before he went home, and when his mother saw green she turned purple with disgust and started to say, "Yuck." But before she could, Bob ran and put his hand on her mouth and held the word in while he traded coats and then removed his hand so she said, "Yay!"

It was at this moment that Bob realized he had a special gift. He could change his colors with ease. With a little practice, he was able to shed one coat and replace it with another in a matter of seconds. Even Bob didn't understand his versatility, but he was pleased with it. For now he could be any color anytime and please every person.

His skill at changing coats quickly elevated him to high positions. Everyone liked him because everyone thought he was just like them. With time he was elected mayor over the entire city.

His acceptance speech was brilliant. Those who loved green thought he was wearing green. Those who loved yellow thought he was wearing yellow, and his mother just knew he was wearing blue. Only he knew that he was constantly changing from one to the other.

It wasn't easy, but it was worth it, because at the end everyone said, "Yay!"

Bob's multicolored life continued until one day some yellow-coated people stormed into his office. "We have found a criminal who needs to be executed," they announced, shoving a man toward Bob's desk. Bob was shocked at what he saw. The man wasn't wearing a coat at all, just a T-shirt.

"Leave him with me," Bob instructed, and the yellow coats left.

"Where is your coat?" asked the mayor.

"I don't wear one."

"You don't have one?"

"I don't want one."

"You don't want a coat? But everyone wears a coat. It, it, it's the way things are here."

"I'm not from here."

"What coat do they wear where you are from?"

"No coat."

"None?"

"None."

Bob looked at the man with amazement. "But what if people don't approve?"

"It's not their approval I seek."

Bob had never heard such words. He didn't know what to say. He'd never met a person without a coat. The man with no coat spoke again.

"I am here to show people they don't have to please people. I am here to tell the truth."

If Bob had ever heard of the word *truth*, he'd long since rejected it. "What is truth?" he asked.

But before the man could answer, people outside the mayor's office began to scream, "Kill him! Kill him!"

A mob had gathered outside the window. Bob went to it and saw the crowd was wearing green. Putting on his green coat, he said, "There is nothing wrong with this man."

"Yuck!" they shouted. Bob fell back at the sound.

By then the yellow coats were back in his office. Seeing them, Bob changed his colors and pleaded, "The man is innocent."

"Yuck!" they proclaimed. Bob covered his ears at the word.

He looked at the man and pleaded, "Who are you?"

The man answered simply, "Who are you?"

Bob did not know. But suddenly he wanted to. Just then his mother, who'd heard of the crisis, entered the office. Without realizing it, Bob changed to blue. "He is not one of us," she said.

"But, but, . . ."

"Kill him!"

A torrent of voices came from all directions. Bob again covered his ears and looked at the man with no coat. The man was silent. Bob was tormented. "I can't please them and set you free!" he shouted over their screams.

The man with no coat was silent.

"I can't please you and them!"

Still the man was silent.

"Speak to me!" Bob demanded.

The man with no coat spoke one word. "Choose."

"I can't!" Bob declared. He threw up his hands and screamed, "Take him, I wash my hands of the choice."

But even Bob knew in making no choice he had made one. The man was led away, and Bob was left alone. Alone with his coats.

*Study Guide*

. . . . . . .

## CHAPTER ONE
## THE WOODCUTTER'S WISDOM

1.  Think about the woodcutter's story for a minute. How would you have responded to the events of the woodcutter's life? Would you have been quick to draw conclusions or content to see what unfolded?

    Now consider the ways in which you pass judgment on the storms that blow into your own life. Could you benefit from adopting a perspective more like that of the woodcutter than that of the villagers? Explain your answer.

2.  Why do you think it is so easy to pass judgment on life "with only one day's evidence"? What are the dangers of passing judgment too quickly?

3.  Describe a time when you made judgments about a specific circumstance without realizing how limited your perspective really was. What was the result of your judgments? Did your judgments stand the test of time, or prove to be only fragments?

4.  Read Matthew 6:33–34. What do you think Jesus was trying to communicate to his followers through those words? How do those words provide perspective for your life?

# CHAPTER TWO
# THE SWEET SOUND
# OF THE SECOND FIDDLE

*Points to Ponder*

"You've been playing second fiddle for too long. You need to step out on your own."

1. Have you ever received advice like the statement above?

2. Have you ever given such advice? What was the result of acting on such advice?

"Living off the praise of others is an erratic diet."

1. What does the statement above mean?

2. In what way is it an "erratic diet"?

"To this day whenever the sun shines and the moon reflects and the darkness is illuminated, the moon doesn't complain or get jealous. He does what he was intended to do all along; the moon beams."

1. What is the result of doing what you were created to do?

2. Do you know this feeling? Explain.

*Wisdom from the Word*

• Read 1 Corinthians 12:12–30. How could heeding the advice in this passage have saved the moon from a lot of grief? Is there a lesson here for you? If so, what is it?

- Read Romans 12:3–8. How could the advice given in verse 3 have spared the moon some pain? How does it fit in with the guidelines laid out in the rest of the passage?

- Read Isaiah 43:5–7. For what were we created, according to Isaiah? How do we "glorify" God? Are you doing so? Explain.

## CHAPTER THREE
## THE CAVE PEOPLE

### Echoes of Thunder

1. "The sounds in the cave were mournful, but the people didn't know it, for they had never known joy. The spirit in the cave was death, but the people didn't know it, for they had never known life."

   A. How can someone not know their true condition?

   B. What people do you know who are unaware of their true condition?

2. "Light always hurts before it helps," he answered. "Step closer. The pain will soon pass."

   A. Why does "light" always hurt before it helps? What does the light represent in this parable?

   B. How does light finally help? How important is the pain? Explain.

3. "Carry this to your people. Tell them the light is here and the light is warm. Tell them the light is for all who desire it."

A. What is the point of this passage?

B. What light have you been asked to carry to your own people? Who are your own people? Are they seeing light in your hands? Explain.

## Flashes of Lightning

1. Read John 1:3–13.

A. In what way is Jesus our light?

B. How are men prone to respond to this light (verses 10–11)?

C. What promise is given in verses 12–13?

2. Read Romans 1:13–17.

A. What was Paul's goal in verse 13?

B. What was Paul's attitude in verses 14–15?

C. What was Paul's confidence in verses 16–17?

3. Read 1 Corinthians 9:19–23.

A. What was Paul's commitment in verse 19?

B. What was Paul's method in verses 20–22?

C. What was Paul's goal in verse 23?

# CHAPTER FOUR
# THE YAY-YUCK MAN

## Echoes of Thunder

1.  "Now Bob could be any color, any time, and please every person."

    A. If you were asked to pick one word to describe Bob, what would it be? Why would you pick this word?

    B. Why are we sometimes tempted to act like Bob?

2.  "Everyone liked him because everyone thought he was just like them."

    A. Why do we like others who seem just like us?

    B. What is the huge trap concealed in this kind of attitude?

3.  "'It's not their approval I seek,' said the man."

    A. Who does this man represent? Why do you think so?

    B. Whose approval do you seek? Why?

4.  "'I am here to show people they don't have to please people,' the man said. 'I am here to tell the truth.'"

    A. Have you ever felt as if you had to please people? If so, why did you feel this way?

    B. What is the best way of reminding ourselves we don't have to please people?

### Flashes of Lightning

1. Read John 8:39–47.

   A. What truth did Jesus tell the Pharisees? How did they respond?

   B. Why couldn't the Pharisees believe Jesus, according to verse 47?

2. Read Galatians 4:16–18.

   A. What question did Paul ask in verse 16? How might this be possible?

   B. Why did Paul tell them the truth, according to verses 17–18?

3. Read Galatians 1:10.

   A. What question did Paul ask here?

   B. What answer does he give to his own question? What does this imply for us?

# *Notes*

## Chapter 1—The Woodcutter's Wisdom

1. Ecclesiastes 7:8.
2. Romans 12:12.
3. Matthew 6:34.